SO-DXL-917

For Holly

Published in the United States 1991 by
Dial Books for Young Readers
A Division of Penguin Books USA Inc.
375 Hudson Street / New York, New York 10014

Published in Great Britain by J. M. Dent & Sons Ltd.
Text copyright © 1991 by J. M. Dent & Sons Ltd.
Illustrations copyright © 1991 by Claire Henley
All rights reserved / Printed in Italy
First Edition
1 3 5 7 9 10 8 6 4 2

Library of Congress Cataloging in Publication Data
Henley, Claire.
Jungle day / Claire Henley. p. cm.
Summary: Relates how a colorful array of animals in the jungle,
including zebras, leopards, snakes, and monkeys, spends its day.
ISBN 0-8037-0959-5
[1. Jungle animals—Fiction.] I. Title.
PZ7.H3893Ju 1991 [E]—dc20 90-46326 CIP AC

The art for each picture consists of a gouache painting,
which is scanner-separated and reproduced in full color.

Claire Henley

JUNGLE DAY

Dial Books for Young Readers
New York

The sun shines over the jungle.
The trees grow tall and green.

Parrots fly in and out
of the treetops.

Monkeys chatter loudly
and swing from branch to branch.

The leopard walks
through the tall grass.

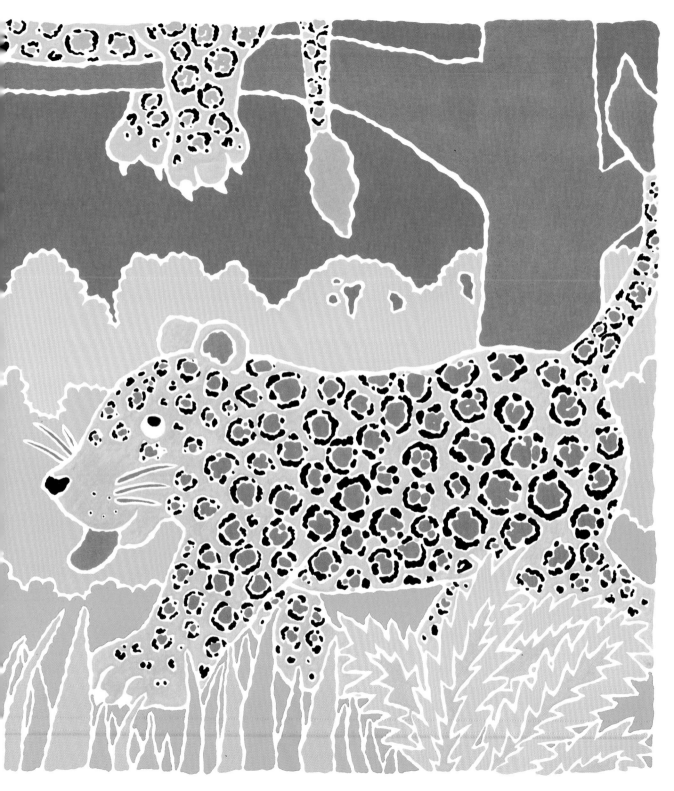

The snake hisses and slithers
to the wide river.

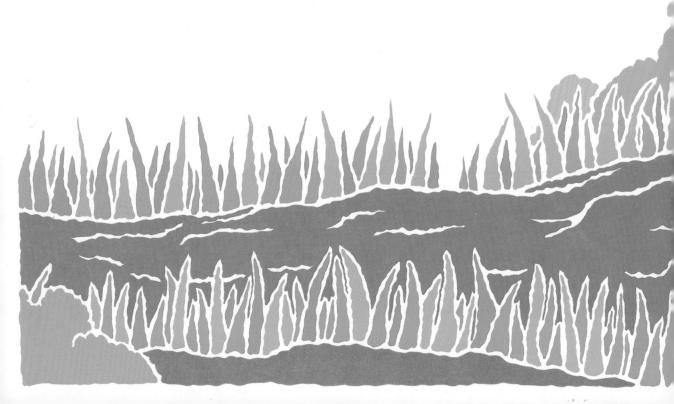

Hippos stand in
the warm black mud.

Elephants squirt water
at each other.

The crocodile snaps
its jaws open and shut.

Zebras run across the plain.

The tall giraffes munch leaves
from the highest branches.

The lion roars
and shakes its mane.

The sun goes down.
The tiger cubs curl up.
Everyone goes to sleep.
Good night.